# QUEEN BEE

## CHYNNA CLUGSTON

An imprint of

📖SCHOLASTIC

New York   Toronto   London   Auckland   Sydney   Mexico City   New Delhi   Hong Kong   Buenos Aires

To my favorite art teacher, Mr. Zimmerman.
Thank you for the encouragement, Mr. Z. Rest in peace.

C.M.

Fort Miller Middle School, Fresno, CA

Lyrics excerpted from: "The Beat," © The Go-Go's, *Beauty and The Beat*,
IRS Records/A&M. All rights reserved.

"Rich Girl." Words and Music by Michael Elizondo, Eve Jeffers, Chantal Kreviazuk,
Andre Young, Gwen Stefani, Kara Dioguardi, Mark Batson, Sheldon Harnick and
Jerry Bock. Copyright © 2004 Music Of Windswept, Blotter Music, Elvis Mambo
Music, Universal Music Corp., Blondie Rockwell, Sony/ATV Music Publishing Canada,
Neverwouldathot Music, WB Music Corp., Ain't Nothing But Funkin' Music,
Harajuka Lover Music, K'Stuff Publishing, Bat Future Music, Mayerling Productions
Ltd. (administered by R&H Music) and Jerry Bock Enterprises. All Rights for Blotter
Music and Elvis Mambo Music Controlled and Administered by Music Of Windswept
All Rights for Blondie Rockwell Controlled and Administered by Universal Music
Corp. All Rights for Sony/ATV Music Publishing Canada and Neverwouldathot Music
Controlled and Administered by Sony/ATV Music Publishing. Used by permission.

Library of Congress Cataloging-In-Publication Data is available.
ISBN 0-439-71572-5 (hardcover) / ISBN 0-439-70987-3 (paperback)

12 11 10 9 8 7 6 5 4 3          05 06 07 08

First edition, September 2005

Cover colors by Guy Major
Lettering by Comicraft & Active Images
Edited by Sheila Keenan
Book design by Richard Amari
Creative Director: David Saylor
Printed in the United States

4

THEN, AS LUCK WOULD HAVE IT, MY BODY DECIDED TO PLAY A REALLY MEAN TRICK ON ME...

REMAIN... CALM...!

IT WENT TOTALLY CRAZY, AND I DON'T JUST MEAN THE NORMAL STUFF THAT HAPPENS TO GIRLS, EITHER—I MEAN, I HAD SOMETHING *EXTRA*-WEIRD GOING ON.

SHRIEK!

SMASH

WHEN I WAS TOO LAZY TO REACH FOR THE REMOTE CONTROL, IT WOULD JUST UP AND *FLOAT OVER* TO ME...

THAT'S WHEN I KNEW SOMETHING PRETTY FREAKY WAS GOING ON.

VWWWP

THINGS STARTED RANDOMLY FLYING AROUND OR BREAKING WHEN I WAS REALLY UPSET.

ONE MORNING I EVEN MANAGED TO LET THE CAT IN THE DOOR WITHOUT GETTING UP FROM THE KITCHEN TABLE!

I WAS WORRIED, SO I TOLD MY MOM WHAT WAS HAPPENING TO ME. SHE TOLD ME I HAD INHERITED THE GIFT OF *PSYCHOKINESIS*, THE ABILITY TO MOVE INANIMATE OR FARAWAY OBJECTS WITH MY MIND.

MEOW?

FLAKES!

"*GIFT?!*" MORE LIKE A CURSE!

I THOUGHT AT ANY MOMENT I'D START HEARING UNCLE BEN FROM SPIDER-MAN TELLING ME THAT "WITH GREAT POWER COMES GREAT RESPONSIBILITY!" I WAS FREAKING OUT! WHY DID I HAVE TO GET SOME LAME, SUPERHUMAN KIND OF POWER?

WHY COULDN'T I JUST BE *NORMAL?*

HONEY, "*NORMAL*" DOESN'T EXIST. JUST DON'T WORRY ABOUT IT SO MUCH, OKAY?

Y-YEAH...

WHY COULDN'T I TIME TRAVEL OR DISAPEAR OR FLY OR SOMETHING? ALL I COULD DO WAS MOVE STUPID STUFF AROUND WITH MY MIND!

WELL, OF COURSE *PSYCHOKINESIS* JUST ADDED TO MY PROBLEMS AT SCHOOL. I COULDN'T CONTROL IT AT ALL, SO I TRIED TO HIDE IT. I THOUGHT IF I IGNORED THE POWER IT'D GO AWAY. YEAH, RIGHT!

I MADE A COUPLE ATTEMPTS TO HANG WITH THE POPULAR GIRLS OR AT LEAST TALK TO THEM, BUT SOMETHING DUMB WOULD ALWAYS HAPPEN.

HALEY, *YOU* COME OVER HERE.

ALL RIGHT!

I HEARD YOU COULD PLAY SOFTBALL PRETTY WELL, SO DON'T LET ME DOWN, OKAY?

I WON'T!

8

THEN ONE DAY MY MOM TOLD ME WE WERE MOVING TO THE CITY. SHE HAD JUST GOTTEN A NEW JOB AS A FASHION WRITER FOR A TEEN MAGAZINE. TALK ABOUT LUCK!

SQUEAL!

MOVING MEANT A NEW SCHOOL, WHERE NO ONE WOULD KNOW ME... WHICH IN TURN MEANT THAT I COULD START OVER, WHICH MEANT I COULD IN THEORY GO FROM *LOSER GIRL* TO COOL GIRL, THE *COOLEST* GIRL IF I PLAYED MY CARDS RIGHT!

BUT HOW?

I IMMEDIATELY STARTED ON MY QUEST. IF I WAS GOING TO RULE MY NEW SCHOOL, I'D HAVE TO KNOW EVERYTHING ABOUT BEING COOL. AND *"EVERYTHING"* IS *A LOT* OF INFORMATION.

I COLLECTED EVERY BIT OF MATERIAL I COULD GET MY HANDS ON. BOOKS, *DVDS*, MAGAZINES, WEBSITES, YOU NAME IT.

I WATCHED EVERY MOVIE EVEN REMOTELY ON THE SUBJECT OF POPULARITY. *PRETTY IN PINK, DROP DEAD GORGEOUS, VALLEY GIRL, JAWBREAKER, MEAN GIRLS*—IT DIDN'T MATTER WHEN THE MOVIE WAS MADE, IT WAS ALWAYS THE SAME PRINCIPLE! ACTING CUTE, DRESSING WELL, AND BEING BLONDE HELPS.

I PRACTICED MY FACIAL EXPRESSIONS IN THE MIRROR AND TRIED TO FIND CUTE WAYS TO POSE WITHOUT LOOKING LIKE I WAS POSING.

HEY, WHAT'S UP?

HOW'S IT GOIN'?

HOLA, MUCHACHAS! (I DON'T EVEN KNOW WHAT THAT MEANS...!)

10

11

IT ALSO EXPLAINS HER HEARING PROBLEMS. PAIGE PLAYS HER MUSIC SO LOUD ALL THE TIME THAT HER EARS RING. SHE ASKS US TO REPEAT EVERYTHING WE SAY ABOUT TWENTY TIMES A DAY!

WHAT?

THIS IS RACHEL: CLASS PREZ, ENTREPRENEUR, AND NATURAL-BORN LEADER. SHE'S ACTUALLY FAR MORE DIPLOMATIC THAN WE LET ON, BUT SHE ALMOST ALWAYS GETS HER WAY NO MATTER WHAT. DIPLOMACY JUST MAKES HER LOOK BETTER WHILE DOING IT.

IN OTHER WORDS, SHE COULD ARGUE THE PANTS OFF ANYONE, MAN.

I'LL BE A LAWYER, NO DOUBT ABOUT IT.

YOU KNOW, BECOMING A LAWYER IS THE FIRST STEP TOWARDS BECOMING A POLITICIAN!

I'M THINKING FIRST LADY PRESIDENT?

FUNNY, THAT'S JUST WHAT I HAD IN MIND!

AND LAST BUT NOT LEAST, THIS IS JETTE. SHE'S GOT A SORT OF NERVOUS DISPOSITION--

SHE'S COMPLETELY PARANOID!

SIIIGH

YEAH. I MEAN, YOU NAME IT--SHE'S PROBABLY FREAKED OUT BY IT. BUT HER NUMBER ONE PARANOIA IS *GERMS*. I SWEAR SHE BATHES IN HAND SANITIZER.

IT'S WEIRD, TOO, BECAUSE HER FAMILY IS NOTHING LIKE THAT. THEY EVEN HAVE A HARD TIME JUST GETTING HER OUT OF THE HOUSE TO GO TO A DANCE AND HAVE FUN!

BUT WE LOVE HER, NERVOUSNESS AND ALL.

HAND SANITIZER

HI, HALEY.

14

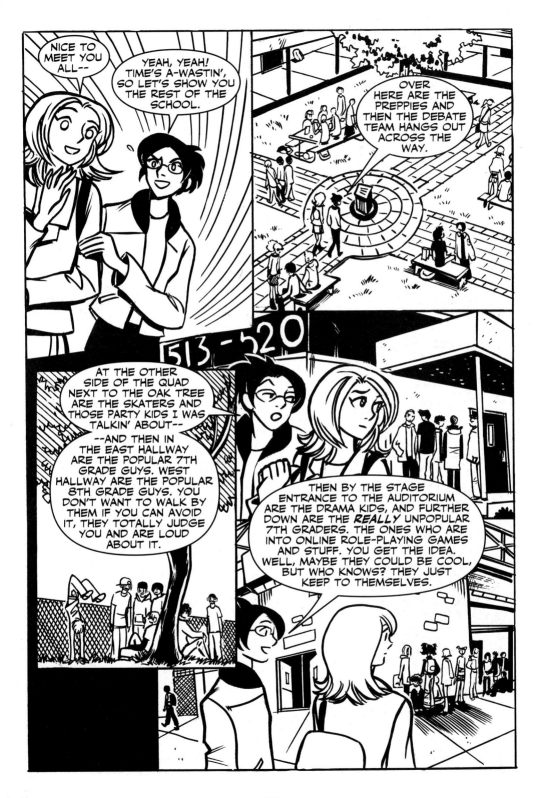

NICE TO MEET YOU ALL--

YEAH, YEAH! TIME'S A-WASTIN', SO LET'S SHOW YOU THE REST OF THE SCHOOL.

OVER HERE ARE THE PREPPIES AND THEN THE DEBATE TEAM HANGS OUT ACROSS THE WAY.

AT THE OTHER SIDE OF THE QUAD NEXT TO THE OAK TREE ARE THE SKATERS AND THOSE PARTY KIDS I WAS TALKIN' ABOUT--

--AND THEN IN THE EAST HALLWAY ARE THE POPULAR 7TH GRADE GUYS. WEST HALLWAY ARE THE POPULAR 8TH GRADE GUYS. YOU DON'T WANT TO WALK BY THEM IF YOU CAN AVOID IT, THEY TOTALLY JUDGE YOU AND ARE LOUD ABOUT IT.

THEN BY THE STAGE ENTRANCE TO THE AUDITORIUM ARE THE DRAMA KIDS, AND FURTHER DOWN ARE THE *REALLY* UNPOPULAR 7TH GRADERS. THE ONES WHO ARE INTO ONLINE ROLE-PLAYING GAMES AND STUFF. YOU GET THE IDEA. WELL, MAYBE THEY COULD BE COOL, BUT WHO KNOWS? THEY JUST KEEP TO THEMSELVES.

AND OVER HERE IS THE CAFETERIA, WHERE JUST ABOUT EVERYONE ELSE HANGS OUT. MOST OF THE JOCKS AND POPULARS ARE IN HERE, THE 7TH AND 8TH GRADE POPULAR GIRLS AND THE WANNABES.

AREN'T THOSE GIRLS IN OUR CLASS?

YEAH.

THAT'S DOMINIQUE, ANJELICA, KEIKO, AND STEFFI. EVERYONE CALLS THEM *"THE HIVE."* THEY'RE DEFINITELY THE MOST POPULAR KIDS AT JFK.

*"THE HIVE?"*

YOU KNOW, LIKE BEES.

FATTENING UP ON THEIR HONEYCOMB WITH THE WHOLE SCHOOL CATERING TO THEM LIKE THEIR OWN PERSONAL *DRONES.*

THEY'RE *VIPERS* IN DESIGNER CLOTHES, HALEY. I'D STAY CLEAR OF THEM IF I WERE YOU.

AW, I'M SURE THEY'RE NOT THAT BAD. *OOOH!* THAT ANJELICA GIRL HAS THAT NEW CELL PHONE!!!

17

I NEEDED TO FIND A WAY TO STAND OUT SO THAT THE HIVE WOULD SEE ME AS SOMEONE THEY'D WANT IN THEIR GROUP, AND FAST. OTHERWISE I'D JUST BE STUCK HANGING OUT WITH TRINI AND HER FRIENDS. NO HOPE OF SUPERPOPULARITY THERE.

THE PROBLEM WAS THAT I COULDN'T FIGURE OUT WHAT KIND OF AMAZING THINGS WOULD GET THAT HIVE BUZZING. UNTIL AFTER SCHOOL...

WHAT'S WRONG?

SOME 7TH GRADER GRABBED MY SNEAKER WHEN I WAS TRYING TO PUT IT ON AND THREW IT INTO THAT TREE! THERE'S NO WAY I CAN GET IT BACK DOWN... AND NOW MY MOM'S GONNA KILL ME! I'LL BE GROUNDED UNTIL I'M EIGHTEEN...

I SEE WHAT YOU MEAN!

WHY DON'T YOU GO WASH OFF YOUR FACE AND I'LL TRY TO GET IT DOWN FOR YOU, OKAY?

'KAY...

18

UUUHN!

LET'S GO!

HOW'D YOU *DO* THAT?!

WHOA! DID YOU *SEE* THAT?

AFTER THAT, THE WHOLE SCHOOL KNEW WHO I WAS. WORD ABOUT MY RESCUE AND LIGHTENING-QUICK MOVES SPREAD FAST VIA IMS AND CELLS. SUDDENLY I'M EVERYBODY'S HERO. EVEN THE 8TH GRADERS ARE IMPRESSED: THEY HATED THAT BULLY, TOO.

THE WHOLE SCHOOL KNEW ABOUT ME NOW... SO DID *THE HIVE*.

...OKAY. SO WHAT DO YOU GUYS THINK ABOUT THAT NEW GIRL?

WELL, SHE HAS REALLY GOOD CLOTHES, AND EVERYONE SEEMS TO LIKE HER...

I HEARD HER MOM IS, LIKE, SOME *BIG FASHION MAGAZINE* BOSS OR SOMETHING. THAT COULD BE SUCH AN IN TO WHAT'S GOING TO BE ON THE RACKS BEFORE THE NEWS EVEN HITS THE GLOSSIES!

WHAT DO *YOU* THINK ANJIE?

COOL! WELL, IN THAT CASE, MY FRIENDS AND I WERE WONDERING IF YOU'D LIKE TO HANG WITH US TOMORROW. I WOULD SAY TODAY, BUT LUNCH IS ALMOST OVER, AND WE BELIEVE IN ALWAYS STARTING AFRESH WITH THE FULL LUNCH HOUR WHEN WE'RE *INTERVI* -- ER, MEETING NEW PEOPLE.

SOUNDS GOOD. SEE YOU TOMORROW!

NEEDLESS TO SAY, I WAS COMPLETELY PREPARED FOR ANY QUESTIONS THEY ASKED ME. THEIR INTERVIEW WENT SOMETHING LIKE:

SHOES, HAIR PRODUCTS, FAVORITE COLORS, MUSIC, AND MOVIES.

SKIN CARE, MAKEUP, BRA SIZE, BOYS, JEANS, MINISKIRTS, AND BRACELETS.

SO HERE I AM, ALL SETTLED INTO THE HIVE. THERE'S ONLY ONE PROBLEM: MY *PSYCHOKINESIS* STILL GOES PSYCHO SOMETIMES!

ZZZAP

AND WHATEVER HAPPENS ALWAYS MAKES ANJELICA LOOK BAD, EVEN THOUGH IT'S TOTALLY NOT MY FAULT!

AAA!

MUST BE A LOT OF... UH... MOISTURE IN THE AIR TODAY!

WAS THAT A BAG OF CHIPS ON HER BACK?

MUST BE A LITTLE STATIC ELECTRICITY IN THE AIR TODAY, TOO.

BRIDE O'FRANKENSTEIN

23

I DON'T KNOW IF SHE TOLD YOU, BUT TRINI AND ANJIE USED TO BE BEST FRIENDS IN ELEMENTARY SCHOOL. INSEPARABLE.

NO WAY, REALLY?

YEAH, TOTALLY. BUT AFTER THEY HIT 7TH GRADE, ANJIE JUST ENDED UP BEING NATURALLY SOCIAL AND POPULAR ALL OF A SUDDEN, SO SHE WANTED TO HANG OUT WITH OTHER PEOPLE. TRINI GOT ALL CLINGY AND JEALOUS 'CAUSE SHE WANTED ANJIE TO HERSELF. ANJIE HAD TO TELL HER TO LEAVE HER ALONE FOR GOOD.

IT'S SAD, REALLY. EVEN NOW YOU CAN TELL SHE HATES US BECAUSE WE'RE CLOSE TO ANJIE AND SHE'S NOT. SHE'LL SAY ANYTHING TO TRY TO MAKE US LOOK BAD.

WOW, I HAD NO IDEA!

AFTER THAT, I STOPPED HANGING OUT WITH TRINI.

I KNOW. YOU CAN HANG OUT WITH HER IF YOU WANT TO, BUT I WOULDN'T BELIEVE ANYTHING SHE SAYS IF I WERE YOU. I MEAN, HOW SELFISH CAN A GIRL BE? AND SOME OF THE THINGS SHE SAYS, THEY'RE JUST SO MEAN!

YEAH...

I ALWAYS MADE AN EXCUSE OR SOMETHING TO BE SOMEWHERE ELSE, AND SOON SHE DIDN'T ASK ME TO DO STUFF ANYMORE. I FELT BAD, BUT THEN I REMEMBERED WHAT KEIKO HAD TOLD ME. WHY WOULD KEIKO LIE? WHAT SHE SAID HAD TO BE TRUE!

SO I'M EXCLUSIVELY HANGING OUT WITH *THE HIVE* NOW, AND EVERYTHING IS GOING ACCORDING TO PLAN. ANJIE HAS STOPPED COMPETING WITH ME ENTIRELY, AND NOW ALL THE GIRLS LOOK TO ME FOR ADVICE. MY OPINION ENDS UP BEING THE FINAL WORD ON EVERYTHING, AND IN THEORY, THIS SHOULD BE GREAT... EXCEPT I DON'T FEEL EXACTLY THE WAY I THOUGHT I WOULD.

I'M BEGINNING TO WONDER IF TRINI WAS ACTUALLY RIGHT: MAYBE I DON'T BELONG IN THIS HIVE.

12:05

LOOK AT HER. THAT GIRL'S BUTT IS WAY TOO BIG FOR THOSE JEANS.

I DON'T EVEN KNOW WHY SAMANTHA PUTS ON MAKEUP. HER SKIN LOOKS LIKE THE SURFACE OF THE MOON! SHE'LL NEVER BE ABLE TO COVER IT ALL UP!

LOOK AT SANDY! THAT GIRL TOTALLY DRESSES LIKE A RETIRED SPICE GIRL!

12:22

I CAN'T BELIEVE YOU THINK TAD IS CUTE. HIS HAIR LOOKS LIKE HE GOES AROUND STICKING FORKS IN POWER SOCKETS!

HOLD UP, HERE COMES THAT WITCH, CAROLINE.

EVERYBODY IS TOTALLY IN LOVE WITH *ALEXA*. EVEN *ANJIE* THINKS SHE'S GREAT. IT'S ALL ALEXA, ALL THE TIME...ALEXA, ALEXA, ALEXA. I'M JUST, LIKE, *"WHATEVER."*

BUT EVEN THOUGH I THOUGHT ALEXA WAS A TOTAL SOCIAL FAKER, I WAS STILL PRETTY EXCITED THAT THERE WAS SOMEONE ELSE AT SCHOOL WITH *PSYCHOKINETIC* ABILITIES, YOU KNOW? MAYBE WE COULD BE *"PSYCHO"* TOGETHER OR SOMETHING. *HA!*

HALEY, IS IT? CAN I TALK TO YOU FOR A SECOND IN MY OFFICE?

SO, YOU'VE GOT IT TOO, HUH? THAT HURRICANE IN CLASS YESTERDAY? I'VE NEVER HAD THAT HAPPEN BEFORE. YOU KNOW WHAT I'M TALKING ABOUT, RIGHT?

UH, YEAH...I DO! WOW, IT'S SO NICE TO FINALLY MEET SOMEONE WITH THE SAME--

YEAH, WHATEVER. LISTEN, I THINK IT *MIGHT* BE A WISE IDEA IF WE MADE SURE STUFF LIKE THAT DIDN'T HAPPEN AGAIN, YOU KNOW? IT CAN'T BE TOO HARD FOR YOU TO CONTROL YOURSELF, IF I CAN DO IT. BUT MAYBE FOR SAFETY'S SAKE, YOU SHOULD STAY OUT OF MY WAY...SO NO ONE GETS *HURT.*

OH, RIGHT... SURE.

AFTER ALL, WE DON'T WANT TO ATTRACT THE *WRONG* KIND OF ATTENTION, DO WE? THOUGHT NOT.

38

42

EITHER WAY, I NEED TO TRY TO GET MY GRADE IN SOCIAL STUDIES BACK UP. IF ONLY I COULD GET MRS. GERSTINE TO LET ME TAKE A MAKEUP TEST!

I CAN'T DO IT, HALEY.

PLEASE? I WANT TO MAKE THIS RIGHT, MRS. GERSTINE. HOW CAN I PROVE I WASN'T TRYING TO CHEAT OTHER THAN BY TAKING A MAKEUP TEST ON THE SAME SUBJECT?

THAT WOULDN'T WORK, EITHER. I CAN'T CHANGE YOUR F NOW..... AT THIS POINT, IT MIGHT AS WELL BE SET IN STONE. I'M SORRY.

I-I UNDERSTAND... I'LL JUST HAVE TO FLUNK OUT OF SCHOOL, I GUESS... GET A PART-TIME JOB OR TWO TO SUPPORT MYSELF... EAT INSTANT RAMEN NOODLES FOR THE REST OF MY LIFE. MAYBE A CHEESE-BURGER ON HOLIDAYS, IF I'M LUCKY...

LOOK, HALEY, IF YOU WANT TO BRING YOUR GRADE BACK TO WHERE IT WAS, WHAT YOU REALLY NEED TO DO IS ACE THIS REPORT COMING UP. WE TALKED ABOUT IT AFTER THE TEST.

THERE'S ONE CATCH, THOUGH -- IT'S NOT A SOLO PROJECT. YOU NEED TO WORK WITH A PARTNER.

A PARTNER?

YES. WELL, ONE YOU'LL GET ALONG WITH. I HAVE YOU SET TO WORK WITH... JASPER REINES.

WHO?

JASPER REINES... THE QUIETEST BOY IN THE 7TH GRADE. I HADN'T REALLY NOTICED HIM BEFORE, NOW THAT I THINK OF IT.

THAT'S HIM IN THE BACK OF THE CLASS THERE. GO AHEAD AND TAKE A SEAT NEXT TO HIM TODAY, SINCE WE'LL BE STARTING TO BRAINSTORM ON REPORT SUBJECTS.

QUIET PLEASE

...

HEY, DID I BUM YOU OUT IN CLASS YESTERDAY?

NOT REALLY. I'VE GOTTEN OFF TO WORSE STARTS WITH PEOPLE BEFORE.

THAT'S COOL. I GUESS IT'S JUST THAT I DON'T LIKE TALKING A WHOLE LOT. EVERYONE ELSE SEEMS TO DO SO MUCH OF IT, IT'S LIKE NO ONE'S A MYSTERY AROUND HERE. PROBLEM IS THAT WHEN I DO TALK, I CAN'T SEEM TO SAY ANYTHING NICE.

WHERE DO YOU WANT TO WORK ON THIS, ANYWAY? THE LIBRARY CLOSES AFTER THREE.

I DON'T KNOW, MY MOM DOESN'T GET HOME UNTIL SEVEN AND I CAN'T HAVE PEOPLE OVER UNLESS SHE'S THERE.

I GUESS WE COULD GO TO MY HOUSE. THERE'S ALWAYS SOMEONE HOME...

...BUT I GOTTA TELL YOU, IT'S NOT EXACTLY AN IDEAL PLACE TO STUDY....

I'M SURE IT'S NOT THAT BAD!

HA HA HA! YOU'RE NOT ALONE, MOST PEOPLE AROUND HERE SEEM TO HAVE POISON DARTS SHOOT OUT THEIR MOUTHS EVERY TIME THEY OPEN 'EM!

WOW, NICE PLACE!

EH.

BRACE YOURSELF. AND KISS THAT WHITE SHIRT GOOD-BYE.

WHAT? WHY?

LONDON CALLING

49

51

WHAT? OH, THIS--! ER, NOWHERE...

WOW, WHERE'D YOU GET THAT? IT LOOKS OLD.

WHY DO YOU HIDE IT?

EH, IT DOESN'T GO WITH ANY OF MY CLOTHES. I CAN'T STAND TAKING IT OFF, THOUGH... IT'S A FAMILY HEIRLOOM.

AN HEIRLOOM, HUH? IS THERE A *STORY* BEHIND IT?

UH, K-KIND OF. IT'S REALLY, UM, LONG-WINDED AND COMPLICATED, THOUGH. MAYBE I'LL TELL IT TO YOU WHEN WE HAVE MORE TIME....

FAIR ENOUGH.

OH MY GOSH! WHAT TIME IS IT? I SHOULD BE GETTING HOME.

NOW? OKAY, WELL, YOU AREN'T WALKING. MY PARENTS WOULDN'T HAVE IT. WE'LL GIVE YOU A RIDE, ALL RIGHT?

59

BUT SOMEHOW ALEXA WAS ONE STEP AHEAD OF ME. EVERY TIME I CAME UP WITH SOMETHING I LIKED, THE NEXT DAY I'D FIND OUT SHE WAS DOING ALMOST THE EXACT SAME THING!

HERE, PUT THIS CD IN!

EXIT

THE PROBLEM IS THAT SHE NEVER STUCK WITH IT!

SONIK JAM

I'D BE THINKING HER NEW ACT WAS FINAL AND FIND ANOTHER ONE FOR MYSELF TO DO, ONLY TO DISCOVER SHE'D CHANGED HERS AGAIN.

AAAGH...! THAT'S MY NEW SONG!

JFK

I COULDN'T EVEN FIND A PLACE AT SCHOOL TO PRACTICE WITHOUT HER SHOWING UP ALMOST IMMEDIATELY TO SEE WHAT I WAS UP TO.

WELL, I'M NOT GOING TO BE INTIMIDATED OUT OF COMPETING! SHE MUST HAVE A NETWORK OF SPIES TAILING ME OR SOMETHING!

I'M JUST GOING TO HAVE TO COME UP WITH MY ROUTINE IN ABSOLUTE SECRECY... SOMEWHERE SAFE FROM PRYING EYES. MAYBE ENTER THE WITNESS PROTECTION PROGRAM FOR ABOUT A WEEK OR SOMETHING. IT'S CLEAR THAT I'M GOING TO HAVE TO GO UNDER-GROUND IN ORDER TO ESCAPE ALEXA!

...OR AT LEAST GO HOME. I THINK I'LL JUST GO WITH THAT, SAVE SOME TIME.

68

I HAVE TO ASK YOU, THOUGH... WHY DO YOU WANT TO HANG OUT WITH ANJELICA AND *THE HIVE* INSTEAD OF GIRLS LIKE TRINI AND HER FRIENDS? YOU GOT ALONG WITH THEM BETTER, FROM WHAT I SAW.

UM... WELL... I-I FOUND OUT THAT TRINI WASN'T AS NICE AS SHE SEEMED. SOMEONE TOLD ME THAT SHE WAS REALLY JEALOUS ALL THE TIME AND STARTED ACTING ALL WEIRD AND SAYING MEAN STUFF ABOUT ANYONE THAT ANJIE TRIED TO HANG OUT WITH.

"SOMEONE" TOLD YOU THAT? DID YOU EVEN THINK ABOUT WHY THEY MIGHT BE TELLING YOU THAT KIND OF STUFF?

YEAH, I MEAN... WELL, I DIDN'T THINK SHE'D LIE TO ME ABOUT SOMETHING LIKE THAT. I THOUGHT SHE WAS MY FRIEND.

IT WASN'T?

NO! TRINI'S REALLY NICE. NOT FAKE NICE, BUT ACTUALLY NICE.

SOUNDS LIKE A LOUSY FRIEND, 'CAUSE IT WASN'T LIKE THAT AT ALL!

ONE OF MY SISTERS KNEW TRINI BACK IN GRAMMAR SCHOOL AND SAYS SHE WASN'T A JEALOUS TYPE AT ALL. ANJIE STOPPED HANGING OUT WITH HER BECAUSE TRINI WASN'T AS *"COOL LOOKING"* AS THE OTHER GIRLS.

ANJIE THOUGHT SHE'D NEVER BE POPULAR IN THE 7TH GRADE HERSELF IF THEY KEPT ON BEING FRIENDS.

ANJIE NEVER CARED HOW TRINI FELT; SHE WAS ALL ABOUT *"BEING POPULAR"* AND LAME STUFF LIKE THAT. TRINI ONLY SEEMED CLINGY BECAUSE SHE DIDN'T WANT TO LOSE HER BEST FRIEND, BUT SHE GAVE UP AFTER ANJIE MADE FUN OF HER IN FRONT OF EVERYONE ON THE PLAYGROUND ONE DAY.

AND THAT'S HOW THAT STUPID RUMOR GOT OUT.

GEEZ...

THANKS TO JASPER, THE QUESTION OF WHAT TO DO FOR THE COMPETITION WAS SOLVED. BUT ONE BIG PROBLEM STILL REMAINED:

WHAT WAS I GOING TO DO ABOUT THE ALEXA INCIDENT?

*"HALEY, HOW COULD YOU?!"*

HEE-HEE

THE FACT WAS THAT JASPER, ALEXA, AND I ALL KNEW I DIDN'T ACTUALLY THROW THE TRAY.

BUT, WE ALSO KNEW THAT THERE WAS NO WAY TO PROVE THAT I DIDN'T, EITHER. I WAS STUCK LOOKING LIKE THE BAD GUY.

THE NEXT DAY.

HI, GUYS.

WHAT DO *YOU* WANT, HALEY? I CAN'T BELIEVE YOU'D EVEN SHOW YOUR FACE AFTER WHAT YOU DID YESTERDAY!

I JUST WANTED TO COME OVER AND APOLOGIZE TO ALEXA.

OH, YEAH? WELL MAYBE SHE DOESN'T WANT TO HEAR ANYTHING OUT OF YOU.

WAIT, WHAT?

*YOU* WANT TO APOLOGIZE TO *ME?*

YES... FOR *BOPPING* YOU UPSIDE THE HEAD WITH THE LUNCH TRAY YESTERDAY. I DIDN'T MEAN FOR ANYTHING TO HIT YOU. I WAS JUST MAD AND THREW IT TO BLOW OFF STEAM.

BUT I WANTED TO MAKE IT UP TO YOU SOMEHOW, SO I BROUGHT YOU A *GIFT.*

OH, PLEASE. I DON'T WANT ANYTHING *YOU* COULD POSSIBLY GIVE ME.

BUT IT'S SPECIAL... MY MOM GOT IT FROM ONE OF THE MAGAZINE'S CLIENTS—IT'S BRAND-NEW, AND *NO ONE ELSE* HAS IT YET.

...IT'S THE ULTRA-NEW PERFUME... *INQUISITIVE.*

85

87

92

95

97

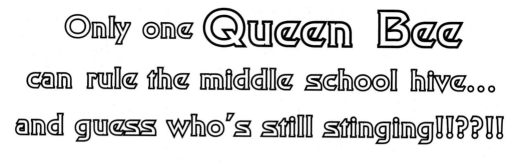

# Only one Queen Bee
## can rule the middle school hive...
## and guess who's still stinging!!??!!

Alexa knows a secret . . .
and Haley is in for a big surprise!

Check out the following pages for a hint about what's next in
*Queen Bee*, the supercool graphic novel series by Chynna Clugston.